HAMTARO™
little hamsters big adventures

WE ARE THE HAM-HAMS!

Learn all about us!

By Frances Ann Ladd
Illustrated by Howard Brower

SCHOLASTIC INC.
New York Toronto London Auckland Sydney
Mexico City New Delhi Hong Kong Buenos Aires

ISBN 0-439-53961-7

HAMTARO ® or ™, the Hamtaro logo, and all related characters and elements are trademarks of Shogakukan Production Co., Ltd.

© R. KAWAI / 2000, 2003 Shogakukan, SMDE, TV Tokyo.
All Rights Reserved.

Published by Scholastic Inc.
SCHOLASTIC and associated logos are trademarks and/or registered trademarks of Scholastic Inc.

Design by Peter Koblish

12 11 10 9 8 7 6 5 4 3 2 1   3 4 5 6 7 8/0

Printed in the U.S.A.
First printing, June 2003

Meet Hamtaro!
He is a brave Ham-Ham.
Ham-Hams are hamster friends.
They have big adventures!

Ham-Hams carry treasures.
Treasures make Ham-Hams special.
"I don't have a treasure," said Hamtaro.
"I want to be special, too.
I will ask my friends for help."

"Hi, Maxwell!" said Hamtaro.
"I need a treasure.
Please tell me about yours!"

"My treasure is a book," said Maxwell.
"Because I love to learn."

ZuZuZu!
Snoozer was asleep again.
"Snoozer's sock must be comfy,"
said Hamtaro.
"I wish I had a comfy treasure."

"Oxnard, you are my best friend,"
said Hamtaro.
"Why do you carry a sunflower seed?"

"I get scared a lot," said Oxnard.
"Sunflower seeds make me feel better.
What makes you feel better?"

"Wow, Sandy!" said Hamtaro.
"That's a great treasure."
"Twirling ribbons is fun," said Sandy.
"You try, Hamtaro!"
"Help?" said Hamtaro.
"My treasure isn't a ribbon."

"Hi, Cappy!" said Hamtaro.
"I like your new hat!
But why do you wear hats?"

"My hats protect me," Cappy said.
"What protects you?"

"Howdy, Howdy!" said Hamtaro.
"I need to find my treasure."
"I like things clean!" said Howdy.
"My treasure is my apron!
It makes me feel ready for my day."

"What do you want?" asked Boss.
"Why do you carry a shovel?" asked Hamtaro.
"I don't have an owner," said Boss.
"It's just me and my shovel.
I depend on this shovel."

"Bijou, your ribbons are pretty,"
said Hamtaro.
"Why do you wear them?"
"My ribbons remind me of home.
They remind me of France," said Bijou.
"But they help me, too.
Once, I used them as bandages!"

"*Hamha!*" said Hamtaro.
"I just love flowers!" said Pashmina.

"Your scarf matches the flowers!"
said Hamtaro. "Is that why you wear it?"
"My scarf keeps me warm," said Pashmina.

"I need to find my treasure," said Hamtaro.
"My treasure is my bow tie," said Dexter.
"It helps me look my best.
What helps you look your best?"

"Hi, Stan!" said Hamtaro.

"Why do you carry maracas?"

"Maracas make me feel happy!" said Stan.

"Cha-cha-cha!"

"What makes me happy?" asked Hamtaro.

"My friends have nice treasures,"
Hamtaro said.
"But I still don't have a treasure."
Hamtaro thought and thought.
"I know!" Hamtaro said.

Hamtaro called for his friends.
"I do have a treasure!" Hamtaro said.
"My Ham-Ham friends!
You are my treasures!
I carry you in my heart."

Hamtaro gave his treasures a hug.